The Wingless Angel

Written by Antonio L. Jocson
& J. E. Christian
Illustrated by Miriam A. Romano

Liberty Bell Production
1180 S. Beverly Dr., Suite 312
Los Angeles, CA 90035

Printed by
Doosan Dong-A Co., Ltd.
Seoul South Korea

ISBN: 1-890963-26-7
Library of Congress No.
97-075526

*O*nce upon a time, long before trains and city lights, an angel came down to earth to take a bath.

She landed, light as a hummingbird, on the rocky bank of a forest pool near a glittering waterfall.

She undressed and took off her wings, laid them on a rock, then stepped into the golden shimmering water.

*A*s she splashed around, a gust of wind came from out of nowhere. It blew her wings onto the limb of an old tree, far beyond her reach.

Kneeling helplessly in the tree's shade, the angel prayed for another puff of wind to send her wings back down to the ground.

The leaves shook with many breezes, but not one was strong enough to free her wings.

"How will I ever get back to heaven now?" she cried.

*I*t so happened that these same breezes carried the sound of her weeping throughout the woods.

The sound slipped through vines and branches until it fell upon the ears of a poor boy gathering charcoal to deliver around town.

The boy's name was Jack. At first he thought the crying was music, for it sounded like beautiful singing.

Jack followed the sound through the forest. He climbed through thickets and trees, lured by the crying song.

Suddenly around a boulder, he saw the pool and sparkling waterfall. At the edge of the pool, he saw the crying angel.

"What's the matter?" Jack asked. He hoped his tattered, sooty clothes would not frighten the girl.

"I've lost my wings up there in the tree," the angel warbled.

Jack was stunned. "Wings?" he repeated.

"Yes, wings," the little girl repeated. "I'm an angel, and a wind blew up there. I can't return to heaven without my wings!"

Jack had never seen an angel before. In fact, he was a little skeptical, for this one looked just like a regular little girl.

"Wait here," he said. He quickly surveyed the tree, shimmied up its trunk and brought down her wings.

Jack thought her wings would be great feathery contraptions, like those on a stork or an albatross. But they weren't at all like a bird's.

*T*he wings were delicate, and lighter than ribbons. They were softer than dandelion tufts, and sparkled more brightly than all the stars at night. He felt as though he were holding magic and love right there in his coal-dirty hands.

"Thank you!" cried the angel joyfully.

Jack put the wings back in her small hands. She put them on.

"You really are an angel!" he said.

"Of course," she answered, "and you are really a good fellow, helping me like that. How can I repay you?"

"Is this where you give me three wishes?" Jack asked.

He remembered a fairy tale about a boy who rubbed a magic lamp and freed a magic genie. The genie granted him three wishes in return.

"I'm only an angel," she said, "I can't give you three wishes. But I can give you one."

"Oh, that's okay," Jack replied. "I really don't need anything."

"But you helped me!" the angel said.

"It was nothing," Jack said bashfully. "I'm just glad I was able to help."

"Please," repeated the angel. "There must be something you want. Please..."

Jack thought for a moment. "Well," he began, "there's going to be a Summer Festival in town, but I have no clothes to wear so I can't go to it."

"Say no more," twittered the angel, "I'll make you a new set of clothes!"

A great smile spread across Jack's face. He was not used to such wonderful surprises. First he met an angel, and now he was going to the festival!

On the way home, Jack and the angel gathered butterfly cocoons and cornflowers, which the angel would use to make the cloth for the suit.

*W*hen they reached his
ramshackle home the angel took off
her wings and began working at a
spindle.

She spun the cocoons and
cornflowers into thread. Then she wove
the thread into cloth. Then she cut the
cloth and sewed it into a magnificent
blue suit.

"Try it on," she chirped.

*J*ack excitedly put on the suit. He was astounded when he looked in the mirror. He saw a tall, handsome fellow, not a poor boy in rags. It was as though he were gazing at the image of someone else. The person he saw was not entirely a stranger. It seemed like someone he had never quite met, but always knew existed.

"Is this me?" he asked the angel in disbelief. "Is this really me?"

The angel laughed a laugh that sounded like a thousand tiny glass bells, ringing. "I don't see anyone else around."

"This is beautiful!"

"This really is you," she said, admiringly. "This is you on the inside."

"I can't believe this is really me," said Jack.

"You will be the envy of the fair!" chimed the angel happily. "Let's go to town so you can see."

The angel left her wings behind so as not to surprise the people.

*N*ever in his wildest dreams had Jack thought he could walk among the finely dressed townsfolk, among all the lords and ladies, bidding them good-day.

He held his head high, for he was dressed as one of them. Everyone marveled at Jack's fabulous suit.

"Where did such a handsome boy come from?" they all wondered.

"I've never seen anyone dress so nicely!" said one.

"Yes," agreed another, "he is even better dressed than Bruno, who usually has the finest clothes around."

*B*runo was the son of the richest man in town. He was a brazen and boastful boy who angered easily when people would not tell him he was the best at this or that, or he had the finest this or that.

Of course, it did not take long before word got to him that there was someone else better than he. His face fired up with anger as he looked everywhere for the boy.

"Point me out this hound!" he commanded.

Bruno's heart sank and blackened at the sight of Jack moving among the admiring crowd in this suit of iridescent, unearthly blue. He had never seen anything so fine in all his life. Bruno looked closer, trying to figure out who it was that could afford such a wonderful garment, for the boy looked a little familiar.

He followed Jack around town, his rage and jealousy building up all the while. Just then, Jack passed a heap of charcoal outside a blacksmith's shop. Then it suddenly hit Bruno.

"This is that poor boy who delivers charcoal to my house!" he murmured under his breath. "How can such a pauper possibly afford such a wonderful suit?" he wondered. "There's something fishy going on here. And who is that little girl with him?"

*M*eanwhile, Jack and the angel spent most of the day walking around town, browsing at the bazaars set up specially for the Summer Festival. There was much joy all around, especially for Jack. He had never been so happy in all his life.

"Thank you again," he said to the angel. "This has been a magical day."

"It is I who should thank you," the angel insisted. "Had you not retrieved my wings I would never have been able to go back to heaven."

When the pair returned to Jack's shack, however, they found that the window had been broken open. Worse yet, the angel's wings were no longer hanging by the window. They were gone.

The angel began to cry again. How would she get back now, she asked Jack. No burst of wind did this. Her wings were not stuck up in some tree. Someone had taken them.

Jack, shocked to his bones, could only wonder, furiously and in vain, who would steal from such a poor boy as he. The whole town knew he had nothing more valuable than the charcoal he delivered for a living.

"Who?" his thoughts cried out. "Who did this?"

*T*he answer came as a knock on the door. It was Bruno. "I, uh... found these things, whatever they are," he snickered. He held up the angel's wings. "You must be missing them, I gather."

"Yes," answered Jack, "and I'll thank you to give them back."

"What do I get in return?" Bruno asked. He held the wings close to him.

Jack was livid. "The wings belong to her. You must return them."

Bruno only looked at him coldly. "I want a reward."

"Or else?" Jack asked.

"Or else it's finder's keepers."

"Please, Jack," the angel said as she stepped forward, "let me give him what he wants so I can be on my way." She turned to Bruno and continued. "What is it that you want?"

Bruno motioned to the spindle in the corner and the spare cuttings of cloth on the floor for Jack's suit.

"I take it you made this boy's suit," he said hotly.

"Yes," the angel replied with a nod, "I did."

"Well, I want you to make me a better one," he sniveled. "I want you to make me the most fabulous suit in all the land, something no one has ever seen before and will never see the likes of again!"

The angel had no choice. "Come back at daybreak," she told Bruno. "Your suit will be ready then."

"Good," Bruno retorted. "And I'll just hold onto these until I get my suit in the morning." And then he left with the wings, whistling maliciously.

"What are we going to do?" Jack asked the angel.

Her brow was furrowed in deep thought, anger or both. She answered without the slightest hint of emotion. "I'll make his suit - something no one has ever seen before and will never see the likes of again."

*T*he angel immediately set off into the woods with Jack in tow.

They went to the darkest parts of the forest where no one went. They went to the places that were the subject of all the scary stories that were told - stories about goblins, ogres and imps, who dragged people down into caves and never let them see the light of the world again. Jack shared some of the stories with her.

"Don't be afraid," said the angel. "There are no such things."

Together, she and Jack gathered all the cobwebs and delicate mosses they could find.

On the way home they gathered delicate yellow mushrooms.

*T*hey brought all of this to the spindle where the angel spun it into thread which she wove into cloth which she sewed into a splendid suit that was indeed finer than the first.

All the while the angel kept repeating. "If he wants a suit that no one has ever seen before and will never see the likes of again, I'll make him a suit."

Bruno came knocking promptly at daybreak, greedily clutching the little angel's wings.

"Where's my suit?" he demanded.

"Your suit," the angel said meekly, "is ready."

"Well let me see it, then!"

Jack pulled aside a small, tattered curtain that revealed the splendid suit. Bruno nearly fell over, for it was indeed the finest thing he had ever seen, all soft and iridescent gold, as though it were not made of cloth at all, but something else, something unearthly. It gleamed like a full moon reflected in the water.

"It's fabulous!" Bruno cawed as he put on the jacket before the mirror. "And I am fabulous! I shall be the best-dressed fellow in all the festival!"

Bruno tossed the angel back her wings and swaggered away to the festival, laughing.

"Come," said the angel, "it's time for you to go to town, too."

"But why?" Jack asked, "everyone will be admiring Bruno."

"Please!" said the angel. She tenderly nudged Jack to the door. "Just go to town."

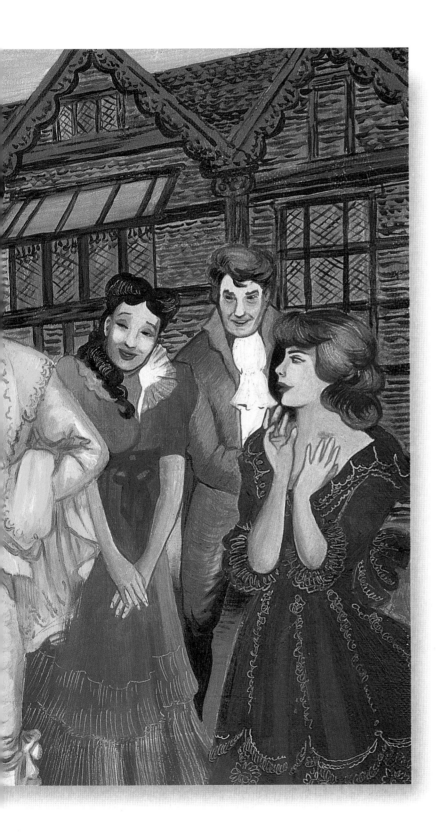

When Jack reached the festival, he saw everyone fawning over Bruno's resplendent suit.

"Ah," they marveled as they crowded around Bruno, "this is even finer than the other boy's."

They snubbed Jack and crowded around Bruno, touching the suit's mysterious cloth.

"This is truly the most fabulous suit in all the world!" Bruno boasted.

"Yes it is!" the crowd agreed. "You are the best dressed fellow at the festival!"

*T*he morning began to warm and brighten. The first sharp rays of the sun flooded the village square, falling upon the thatched rooftops, the cobbled streets, and the fields of sunflowers that lay like a golden sea of the east side of town.

"It's going to be a hot day!" everyone cheered.

"Yes," agreed Bruno. He started noticing something strange about his suit, "it will be a hot day."

*T*he day got warmer. When Bruno touched the fabric, to unbutton a button, the once beautiful material easily came apart in his hands!

His suit began to melt before everyone's eyes, as though it were made of snow, as though it were mist over morning water.

Soon, Bruno was naked! There he stood in the middle of the square, the whole town around him laughing.

"What a suit!" they all cried out in derision, "he cheated with a cheap suit."

They laughed and laughed, as Bruno ran home.

*A*mid the raucous laughter no one heard a tinkling giggle high in the air. No one except Jack. He knew it was the angel, but when he turned to see her, she was gone.

He only saw a bright dot of light, like a comet moving through the morning. It disappeared into the blue sky, back to heaven.

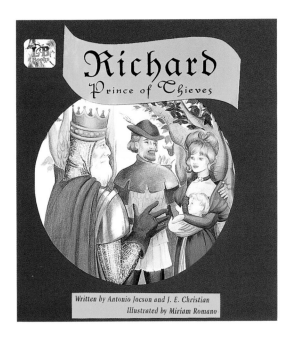

Written by Antonio Jocson and J. E. Christian
Illustrated by Miriam Romano

Richard, Prince of Thieves

Continuing in the tradition of Robin Hood, its namesake, Richard, Prince of Thieves, focuses on Richard, the only son and heir to Robin's reputation. Pitted against the evil Ice Witch, Richard must defend the peaceful village of Holderness from being enslaved by her powerful magic. Armed with only his ingenuity, Richard must rid the village of the witch and her minions once and for all.

Geared for children ages 8 to 11, the illustrated novella charts the coming-of-age story of a boy who must finally confront his doubts about living up to his father's mantle of expectations and fulfill his own destiny.

ISBN NO. 1-890963-25-9   Price $24.50

The Children's Crusade

It is the time of the Crusade and Religious fervor is sweeping Europe. Led by a charismatic boy who claims to have been commanded by God to free the Holy Land, thousands of children board ships bound for Jerusalem. Or so they think. One of those kids, the son of a French Nobleman who fought in the crusade, but is missing and believed dead.

The Children's Crusade chronicles the boy's trials - being sold into slavery and escaping - to find his father against all odds, and safely bring him back home.

ISBN NO. 1-890963-27-5   Price $22.50

The Children's Crusade

Antonio Jocson
J.E. Christian

Liberty Bell Productions

1180 S. Beverly Dr., Ste. 312, Los Angeles, CA 90035